NICOLA BAYLEY & WILLIAM MAYNE

# THE
# MOULDY

JONATHAN CAPE
THIRTY BEDFORD SQUARE
LONDON

For Jeremy Hume  NB

To Talitha, from her boy  WM

British Library Cataloguing in Publication Data

Mayne, William
The mouldy.
I. Title  II. Bayley, Nicola
823′914 (J) PZ7
ISBN 0 224 02092 7

Printed in Italy by A. Mondadori Editore, Verona

First published 1983
Text copyright © 1983 by William Mayne
Illustrations copyright © 1983 by Nicola Bayley
Jonathan Cape Ltd, 30 Bedford Square, London WC1

In the great garden of the world there was peace before Mouldy came. He came from the Wilderness in the night, under the ground, lifting the grass, plowing among the flowers. He shook the king's crystal palace. Along the street he tumbled people from their beds.

They went to the palace and said, "A thing has been along the garden. It has toppled all our houses."

"It has cracked my crystal roof," the king replied. The bees brought honey to him from the flowers of the throne.

Talitha, the daughter of the king, said, "The Daffodil School has fallen down."

"We heard a monster growling in the earth," cried an old Rootwife. "It snapped its teeth."

"There, there," an old hedgehog said, a royal nanny.

"Hear the worst," said the king. "Mouldy intends to spoil the great garden and leave it lost and wild."

He sent Soldiers of the Thistle
to drive Mouldy to the Wilderness
again. All day among the flowers
they did not find him.

At night, while they slept,
Mouldy came a second time,
trampling roots of orchard trees
to make them drop their fruit,
wrinkling garden paths so people
could not walk.

Children found a hole by the
Daffodil School. In it they heard
Mouldy pace back and forth, with
grunt and snarl and snap of teeth.
Talitha took the children to the king.

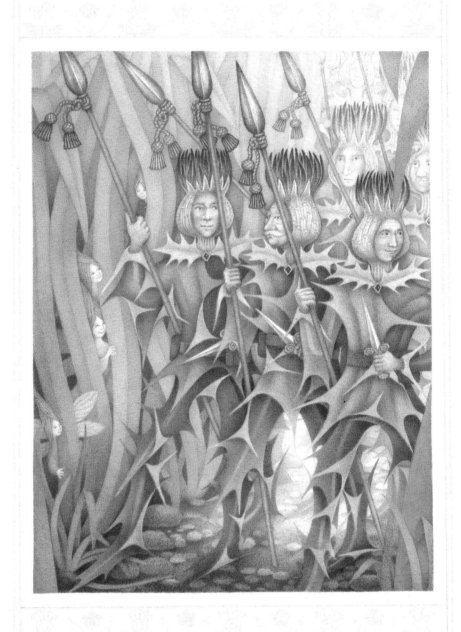

He sent Soldiers of the Thistle
down the hole. The people waited.
Rootwives brewed a victory punch,
and made golden honey-cakes.
Children stitched tapestry with
patterns of the winners marching
home.

But winners did not come
marching home. No one came.
The punch grew sour, honey-cake
turned black, tapestry unravelled
on the floor.

"He'll eat them all," the old hedgehog said. "Soldier by soldier. If I was young I'd deal with him myself."

No one listened to her. In the garden there was sadness. The bees stopped buzzing, birds did not sing, nor flowers open. In the crystal palace silence reigned all day.

Talitha caught a beetle by his black back leg to ask what gossip came from underground. She tied embroidery thread around his neck to hold him.

"Mouldy's underground," said the beetle, "and I'm off to the Wilderness. Now he's here it's safer there."

Talitha sat with a passing slug and spoke to her, looping knitting wool around her horns to wind the ball.

"He has a pantry full of soldiers," said the slug. "People like him never have enough, and I'm tasty but not hasty, so I'm off."

Talitha came to the Daffodil
School and the hole in the ground.
She knew what to do.

She went down the hole, and
walked along the shadows. She
shouted, "Mouldy, Mouldy, come here."

"Go home," said a tiny Rootchild
in the tunnel wall.

"No!" said Talitha. She took out
her needles and began to knit, stitch,
stitch, stitch, bravely in the dark.

Far away she heard the soft
gigantic tread of Mouldy, walking
his tunnel. She heard him sniff
and grunt.

The daughter of a king is not afraid; the eldest child of the Daffodil School cannot tremble. "I'll fight to get our soldiers back," she said.

"You fight," said Mouldy, "I'll bite," and snapped his teeth. They sounded large.

"Excuse me," said Talitha, and punched him on the nose.

"That's nice," said Mouldy. "That's friendly. Rub my nose again, good and hard."

"I won't tickle," said Talitha, and jabbed him with her knitting needles.

"How kind you are," said Mouldy.

"You won't like this," said Talitha, and taking out her embroidery she stuck the crewel needle in.

"Sensational," said Mouldy. "The others ran away, but you have been most welcoming."

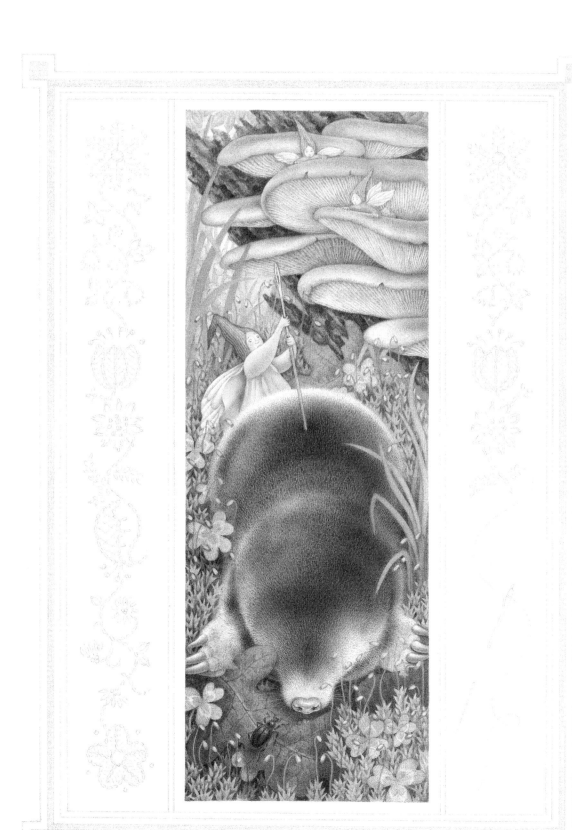

"I think I've won," said Talitha. "Give back all Soldiers of the Thistle in your pantry."

"I'll do anything you say," said Mouldy.

"And leave the garden of the world," said Talitha.

"I'd go anywhere you want," said Mouldy. "You'll marry me, of course."

"I suppose I must," said Talitha. "I've been at school quite long enough, and I have to get the soldiers back."

"Keep scratching," said Mouldy.

"This is going to be hard work," said Talitha.

They set the Soldiers of the Thistle free, and marched with them to the crystal palace.

"I'm not losing a daughter," said the king, "but gaining a Mouldy." He ordered the children of the Daffodil School to be bridesmaids and pages, and dropped a dewy tear.

The hedgehog said, "A royal wedding's always fun. But I should have gone to sort him out. He's more my kind."

"Hedgehog dear," said Talitha, "scratch him while I put on my wedding dress."

"Of course, there, there," said the hedgehog, and she leaned on Mouldy with her spiny side.

"Oh," said Mouldy. "Oh, oh, oh. You make a fellow happy. I think I'd rather marry you."

"There, there," said the hedgehog, brushing him so hard his hair stood on end.

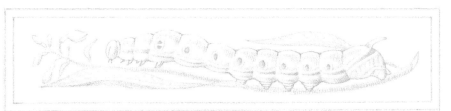

Talitha came back in her
wedding dress of fallen petals.
She was the daughter of a king,
and did not flinch from marrying
Mouldy and living in the far
Wilderness, though she loved him
not at all.

"I hope you will not be upset,"
the hedgehog said. "He has changed
his mind. It's easy work for me to
keep him comfy; and I think I'll
make a better bride."

"Mouldy has no manners," said
the king. "But I am rather pleased.
They can have the royal wedding."

And so they did. After it
there was a long procession to the
far Wilderness.

There, by dusky candlelight,
Talitha kissed the bride goodbye,
and waved her out of sight.

Every year a little old lady
hedgehog comes up from the
Wilderness for a gossip. Mouldy
stays at home, scratching his own
back for a time.

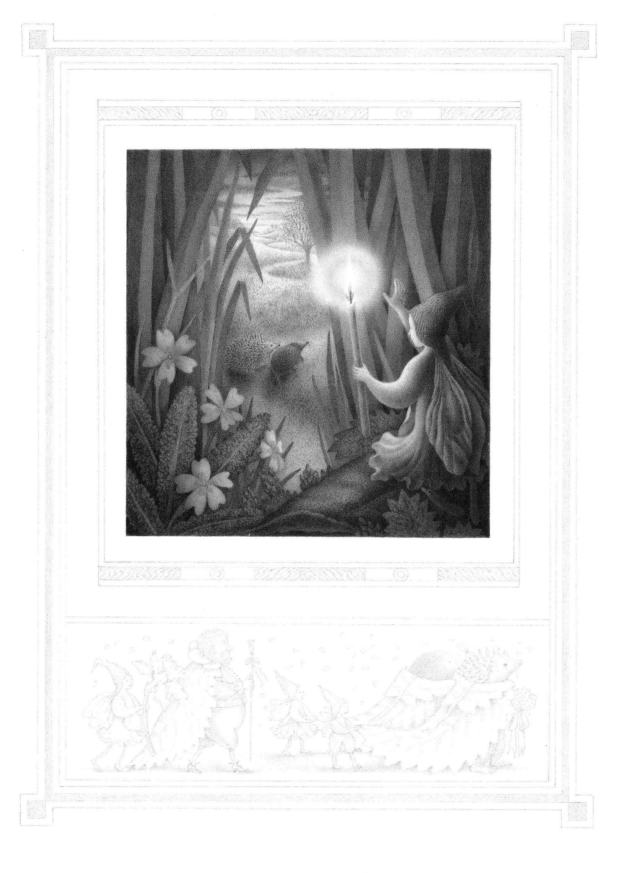

In the end Talitha married a
Fritillary Prince. And always there
is work to do in the great garden
of the world.